MW01118529
Especially for Jan
Hold hands... ma
difference,
Michele P. Hottauer
"2007"

Couldn't We Make a Difference?

To every child

Couldn't We Make a Difference?

Story and Illustrations by

Michele Pace Hofbauer

GREENE BARK PRESS

Publisher's Cataloging-in-Publication
(Provided by Quality Books, Inc.)
Third Printing

Hofbauer, Michele Pace.
Couldn't we? make a difference / written and illustrated by Michele Pace Hofbauer. - Ist ed.
p. cm.
SUMMARY: Children consider what life would be like if everyone could get along, despite differences.
LCCN: 00-132341
ISBN: 1-88085-162-8
Printed in China
1. Race relations—Juvenile fiction.
2. Cooperation—Juvenile fiction.
3. Stories in rhyme. I. Title.

PZ8.3.H643 Cou 2000 [E]
QBI00-470

Born in the heart of every child
Is the power to change the world.

Couldn't we sit down together,
For a while under a tree?
We could watch the clouds
Or look at the stars,
Just think of how nice it would be.

If we could just look at each other,
With eyes that see within,

We'd look past unimportant things,
Like color, clothes and skin.

We'd see we're not so different,
And wouldn't it be fine,

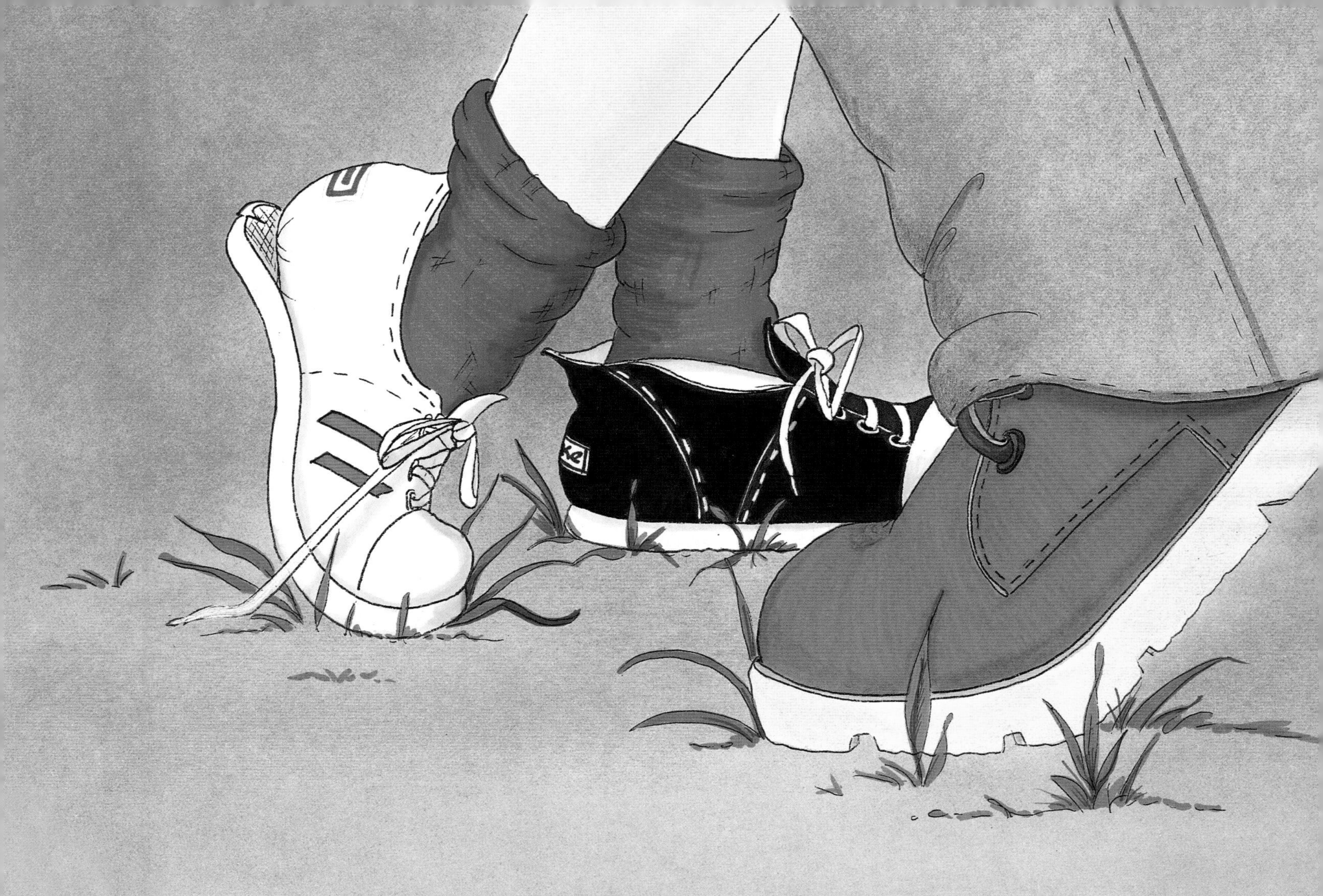

If I could walk in your shoes,
And you could walk in mine?

Couldn't we talk to each other,
Instead of having a fight?
Forget about who's to blame,
Forget who's wrong or right.

Then we could really listen,
To what each of us had to say,
We might find we understand,
Why, we might find a way . . .

To share our secret thoughts and dreams,
Ideas and feelings too,
I think that I could learn a lot,
Listening to you.

Couldn't we play together?
And wouldn't it be fun,
If, to our surprise, no one lost,
And EVERYBODY won?

We wouldn’t ever have to prove,
By race or time or test,
Who’s stronger, faster, smarter,
Bigger or the best.

Couldn't we build together?
A castle, a fort and then,
You never know, I bet it's so,
Perhaps we'd end up friends.

DAIRY
SUNNYSIDE
GOLDEN

Couldn't we fix it together,
Yes, that's what we'll do,
We'll paint it,
Clean it,
Patch it right up,
Why, it'll be good as new.

There is a job that's ours, you know,
One of unbounded worth,

To care for mountains, sea and sky,
And creatures of the earth.

Then, couldn't we help each other,
To walk or climb or stand?
I could give you a leg up,
You could give me a hand.

Couldn’t we love one another,
When we’re tired, hungry and cold,
I’d care for you, you’d care for me,
When we’re lost or troubled or old.

Couldn’t we live together?
We really must decide.

There could be sweet peace on earth,
If we lived side by side.

Each of us could have a say,
We all have the right, you see,
To share a voice heard around the world,
That says, "All of us are free."

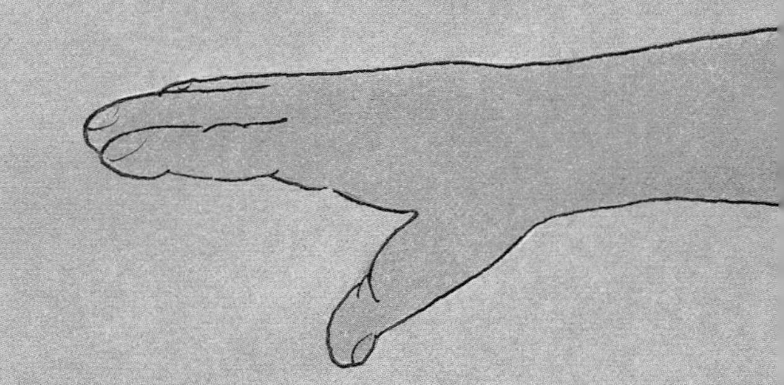

Couldn’t we? Shouldn’t we?
Just think of how nice it would be,
If just for one moment, all of us,
Believed that we could . . .

Couldn’t we?

Note

Note

Note